Firefighter Ted

by Andrea Beaty and Pascal Lemaitre

MARGARET K. McELDERRY BOOKS

NEW YORK   LONDON   TORONTO   SYDNEY

To Katie, who amazes me
—A. B.

For firefighters everywhere,
especially those who gave their
all on September 11, 2001
—P. L.

Margaret K. McElderry Books
An imprint of Simon & Schuster
Children's Publishing Division
1230 Avenue of the Americas
New York, New York 10020
Text copyright © 2009 by Andrea Beaty LLC
Illustrations copyright
© 2009 by Pascal Lemaitre
All rights reserved, including the right of
reproduction in whole or in part in any form.
Book design by Ann Bobco
The text for this book is set in Bliss.
The illustrations for this book are rendered
in brush and ink, then colored digitally.
Manufactured in China
1 2 3 4 5 6 7 8 9 10
Library of Congress Cataloging-in-
Publication Data
Beaty, Andrea.
Firefighter Ted / Andrea Beaty ; illustrated by
Pascal Lemaitre.—1st ed.
p. cm.
Summary: When Ted awakens to the smell
of smoke and cannot find a firefighter,
he decides to become one for the day,
much to the dismay of his mother,
neighbors, principal, and classmates.
ISBN: 978-1-4169-2821-8
[1. Fire fighters—Fiction. 2. Schools—Fiction.
3. Imagination—Fiction. 4. Humorous stories.]
I. Lemaître, Pascal, ill. II. Title.
PZ7.B380547Fir 2009
[E]—dc22
2008031904

FIRST
EDITION

One morning
Ted woke up
and sniffed the air.
It smelled like smoke.

That's not good, thought Ted. *I need a firefighter!*

Ted looked everywhere, but he couldn't find one.

And since Ted couldn't find a firefighter . . .

. . . he became a firefighter.

But every firefighter needs a fire truck.

Firefighter Ted found a fire truck!
That was lucky, he thought.
I need a fire extinguisher, too.

Firefighter Ted looked
everywhere else.

Since he couldn't find a fire extinguisher, he made one.

Now, where is that fire?
thought Firefighter Ted.

Firefighter Ted searched the house.
The kitchen was filled with smoke.
It rose from a plate on the table.

"Stand back!" shouted
Firefighter Ted. He put
out the toast and helped
his mother to safety.

"That was your breakfast,"
said his mother.

"It still is," said Firefighter Ted,
"and now it's nutritious *and* safe."

"Go to school," said his mother.

"Remember," said Firefighter
Ted, "only *you* can prevent
breakfast fires."

It was very hot outside. The sidewalk sizzled and hurt Firefighter Ted's feet. He saw a kitten on the hot sidewalk. It needed help.

Firefighter Ted rescued the kitten . . .

and two puppies . . .

and three tricycles.

The crowd was speechless.

"No need to thank me," said Firefighter Ted, and he waved to the crowd.

When Firefighter Ted arrived at school,
the principal was waiting for him in the hallway.
"You are late," said Principal Bigham.

ALARM

Firefighter Ted frowned.
"You are blocking the fire alarm,"
he said . . .

. . . and he helped the principal to safety.
Principal Bigham turned bright red.
"Watch out!" said Firefighter Ted.
"You're overheating!"

Principal Bigham's face turned redder and redder still.
"Stop, drop, and roll!" said Firefighter Ted, and he helped
Principal Bigham to safety again.

Principal Bigham was speechless. He pointed to
Mrs. Johnson's room.

"No need to thank me,"
said Firefighter Ted.

Mrs. Johnson's students were in line at the door. They were going to see the science fair exhibits in the cafeteria.

"A parade!" shouted Firefighter Ted.
"Firefighters always lead parades!"
Firefighter Ted led the parade down the hall.
"Whoooooo-whoooooo-whooooo!"

All the other classes came
out to watch.
"Everyone loves a parade,"
said Firefighter Ted, and he
waved to the crowd.

Firefighter Ted looked around the cafeteria.
There was danger everywhere!

"VOLCANOES!" yelled Firefighter Ted.

He jumped into action.

Firefighter Ted stopped the volcanoes from erupting and helped the students to safely.

They were speechless.

"No need to thank me,"
said Firefighter Ted.

Suddenly, Firefighter Ted
smelled something burning.

A thin stream of smoke rose from Principal Bigham's pants.

The smoke got thicker and thicker. His pants got hotter and hotter.
Principal Bigham ran this way and that. "HELP!" he yelled.
"Call a tailor! Call the janitor! Call the library!

But Firefighter Ted was already there.

He helped the principal to safety.

He pulled the fire alarm and started the fire sprinklers.

Just then, the tailor arrived with
the janitor and a librarian.
"You need pants," said the tailor.
"And a mop," said the janitor.

"Good thing you had Firefighter Ted," said the librarian.

"My work here is done," said Firefighter Ted. "You can keep the fire extinguisher. And remember . . .

only *you* can prevent pants fires."

That night Ted put away his fire truck and went to bed knowing
he had done a good job. He lay awake for a very long time.
There is so much to know about fire safety, he thought. *A poster
could help everyone understand.*

Ted did not have a poster.
But I could make one, he thought, . . . *if I had a paintbrush.*

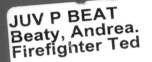